George Tomkyns Chesney

The Fall of England. The Battle of Dorking

Anatiposi

George Tomkyns Chesney

The Fall of England. The Battle of Dorking

Reprint of the original, first published in 1871.

1st Edition 2023 | ISBN: 978-3-38212-456-4

Anatiposi Verlag is an imprint of Outlook Verlagsgesellschaft mbH.

Verlag (Publisher): Outlook Verlag GmbH, Zeilweg 44, 60439 Frankfurt, Deutschland
Vertretungsberechtigt (Authorized to represent): E. Roepke, Zeilweg 44, 60439 Frankfurt, Deutschland
Druck (Print): Books on Demand GmbH, In de Tarpen 42, 22848 Norderstedt, Deutschland

The Fall of England?

"The writer, living about 1925, gives his son an account of his adventures as a Volunteer during the invasion of England fifty years before, and so powerful is the narrative, so intensely real the impression it produces, that the coolest disbeliever in panics cannot read it without a flush of annoyance, or close it without the thought that after all, as the world now stands, some such humiliation for England is at least possible." * * * * "If the writer is, as reported, Col. Hamley, then Col. Hamley, when he wrote the charming story of "Lady Lee's Widowhood," misconceived, as a novelist, the nature of his own powers. He should rival Defoe, not Anthony Trollope."

—London "*Spectator*," *May* 13, 1871.

The Fall of England?

THE BATTLE OF DORKING:

REMINISCENCES OF A VOLUNTEER.

———◆◆◆———

By a Contributor to " Blackwood."

———◆◆◆———

NEW YORK:

G. P. PUTNAM & SONS,

ASSOCIATION BUILDING, TWENTY-THIRD STREET.

1871.

Lange & Hillman, Printers and Stereotypers
108 to 114 Wooster St., N. Y.

THE BATTLE OF DORKING:

REMINISCENCES OF A VOLUNTEER.

———•◆•———

YOU ask me to tell you, my grand-children, something about my own share in the great events that happened fifty years ago. 'Tis sad work turning back to that bitter page in our history, but you may, perhaps, take profit in your new homes from the lesson it teaches. For us in England, it came too late. And yet we had plenty of warnings, if we had only made use of them. The danger did not come on us unawares. It burst on us suddenly, 'tis true, but its coming was foreshadowed plainly enough to open our eyes, if we had not been wilfully blind. We English have only ourselves to blame for the humiliation which has been brought on the land. Venerable old age! Dishonorable old age, I say, when it follows a manhood dishonored as ours has been. I declare, even now, though fifty years have passed, I can hardly look a young man in the face when I think I am one of those in whose youth happened this degradation of Old England—one of those who betrayed the trust handed down to us unstained by our fore-fathers.

What a proud and happy country was this fifty years ago! Free trade had been working for more than a quarter of a century, and there seemed to be no end to the riches it was bringing us. London was growing bigger and bigger; you could not build houses fast enough for the rich people who wanted to live in them, the merchants who made the money, and came from all parts of the world to settle there, and the lawyers, and doctors, and engineers and others, and trades-people, who got their share out of the profits. The streets reached down to Croydon and Wimbledon, which my father could remember quite country places; and people used to say that Kingston and Reigate would soon be joined to London. We thought we could go on building and multiplying for ever. 'Tis true, that even then there was no lack of poverty; the people who had no money went on increasing as fast as the rich, and pauperism was already beginning to be a difficulty; but if the rates were high, there was plenty of money to pay them with; and as for what were called the middle classes, there really seemed no limit to their increase and prosperity. People in those days thought it quite a matter of course to bring a dozen children into the world—or, as it used to be said, Providence sent them that number of babies; and if they couldn't always marry off all the daughters, they used to manage to provide for the sons, for there were new openings to be found in all the professions, or in the Government offices, which went on steadily getting larger. Besides, in those days young men could be sent out to India, or into the army or navy; and even then emigration was not uncommon, although not the regular custom it is now. Schoolmasters, like all other professional classes, drove a capital trade. They did not teach very much, to be sure, but new schools with their four or five hundred boys were springing up all over the country.

Fools that we were! We thought that all this wealth and prosperity were sent us by Providence, and could not stop coming. In our blindness, we did not see that we were merely a big workshop, making up the things which came from all parts of the world; and that if other nations stopped sending us raw goods to work up, we could not produce them ourselves. True, we had in those days an advantage in our cheap coal and iron; and had we taken care not to waste the fuel, it might have lasted us longer. But even then there were signs that coal and iron would soon become cheaper in other parts; while as to food and other things, England was not better off than it is now. We were so rich simply because other nations from all parts of the world were in the habit of sending their goods to us to be sold or manufactured; and we thought that this would last forever. And so, perhaps, it might have lasted, if we had only taken proper means to keep it; but, in our folly, we were too careless even to insure our prosperity, and after the course of trade was turned away it would not come back again.

And yet, if ever a nation had a plain warning, we had. If we were the greatest trading country, our neighbors were the leading military power in Europe. They were driving a good trade, too, for this was before their foolish communism (about which you will hear when you are older) had ruined the rich without benefitting the poor, and they were in many respects the first nation in Europe; but it was on their army that they prided themselves, most—and with reason. They had beaten the Russians, and the Austrians, and the Prussians too, in by-gone years, and they thought they were invincible. Well do I remember the great review held at Paris by the Emperor Napoleon, during the great Exhibition, and how proud he looked showing off his splendid Guards to the assembled kings and princes. Yet three years afterwards, the force so long deemed the first in Europe was ignominiously beaten, and the whole army taken prisoners. Such a defeat had never happened before in the world's history; and with this proof before us of the

folly of disbelieving in the possibility of disaster, merely
because it had never happened before, it might have
been supposed that we should have the sense to take the
lesson to heart. And the country was certainly roused
for a time, and a cry was raised that the army ought to
be reorganised, and our defences strengthened against
the enormous power for sudden attacks which it was
seen other nations were able to put forth. But our Government had come into office on a cry of retrenchment,
and could not bring themselves to eat their own pledges.
There was a radical section of their party, too, whose
votes had to be secured by conciliation, and which
blindly demanded a reduction of armaments as the price
of allegiance. This party always decried military estab-
lishments as part of a fixed policy for reducing the influence of the Crown and the aristocracy. They could not
understand that the times had altogether changed, that
the Crown had really no power, and that the Government merely existed at the pleasure of the House of
Commons, and that even Parliament-rule was beginning
to give way to mob-law. At any rate, the Ministry
were only too glad of this excuse to give up all the
strong points of a scheme which they were not really in
earnest about. The fleet and the Channel, they said,
were sufficient protection. So the army was kept down,
and the militia and volunteers were left untrained as before, because to call them out for drill would "interfere
with the industry of the country.." We could have
given up some of the industry of those days forsooth,
and yet be busier than we are now. But why tell you
a tale you have so often heard already? The nation,
although uneasy, was misled by the false security its
leaders professed to feel; the warning given by the dis-
asters that overtook France was allowed to pass by un-
heeded. The French trusted in their army and in its

great reputation; we in our fleet; and in each case the result of this blind confidence was disaster, such as our forefathers in their hardest struggles could not have even imagined.

I need hardly tell you how the crash came about. First, the rising in India drew away a part of our small army; then came the difficulty with America, which had been threatening for years, and we sent off ten thousand men to defend Canada—a handful which did not go far to strengthen the real defences of that country, but formed an irresistible temptation to the Americans to try and take them prisoners, especially as the contingent included three battalions of the Guards. Thus the regular army at home was even smaller than usual, and nearly half of it was in Ireland to check the talked-of Fenian invasion fitting out in the West. Worse still— though I do not know it would really have mattered as things turned out—the fleet was scattered abroad; some ships to guard the West Indies, others to check privateering in the Chinese seas, and a large party to try and protect our colonies on the Northern Pacific shore of America, where, with incredible folly, we continued to retain possessions which we could not possibly defend. America was not the great power forty years ago that it is now; but for us to try and hold territory on her shores which could only be reached by sailing round the Horn, was as absurd as if she had attempted to take the Isle of Man before the independence of Ireland. We see this plainly enough now, but we were all blind then.

It was while we were in this state, with our ships all over the world, and our little bit of an army cut up into detachments, that the Secret Treaty was published, and Holland and Denmark were annexed. People say now that we might have escaped the troubles which came on us if we had at any rate kept quiet till our other difficulty was settled; but the English were always an impulsive lot: the whole country was boiling over with indignation, and the Government, egged on by the press, and going with the stream, declared war. We had always got out of scrapes before, and we believed our old luck and pluck would somehow pull us through.

Then, of course, there was bustle and hurry all over the land. Not that the calling up of the army reserves caused much stir, for I think there were only about 5,000 altogether, and a good many of these were not to be found when the time came; but recruiting was going on all over the country, with a tremendous high bounty, 50,000 more men having been voted for the army. Then there was a ballot bill passed for adding 55,000 men to the militia; why a round number was not fixed on I don't know, but the Prime Minister said that this was the exact quota wanted to put the defences of the country on a sound footing. Then the shipbuilding that began! Ironclads, despatch-boats, gunboats, monitors,—every building-yard in the country got its job, and they were offering ten shillings a-day wages for anybody who could drive a rivet. This didn't improve the recruiting, you may suppose. I remember, too, there was a squabble in the House of Commons about whether the artisans should be drawn for the ballot, as they were so much wanted, and I think they got an exemption. This sent numbers to the yards; and if we had had a couple of years to prepare instead of a couple of weeks, I daresay we should have done very well.

It was on a Monday that the declaration of war was announced, and in a few hours we got our first inkling of the sort of preparation the enemy had made for the event which they had really brought about, although the actual declaration was made by us. A pious appeal to the God of battles, whom it was said we had aroused, was telegraphed back; and from that moment all communication with the north of Europe was cut off. Our embassies and legations were packed off at an hour's notice, and it was as if we had suddenly came back to the middle ages. The dumb astonishment visible all over London the next morning, when the papers came out void of news, merely hinting at what had happened, was one of the most startling things in this war of surprises. But everything had been arranged beforehand; nor ought we to have been surprised, for we had seen the same Power, only a few months before, move down half a million of men on a few days' notice, to conquer the greatest military nation in Europe, with no more fuss than our War Office used to make over the transport of a brigade from Aldershot to Brighton—and this, too, without the allies it had now. What happened now was not a bit more wonderful in reality; but people of this country could not bring themselves to believe that what had never occurred before to England could ever possibly happen. Like our neighbors, we became wise when it was too late.

Of course the papers were not long in getting news—even the mighty organization set at work could not shut out a special correspondent; and in a very few days, although the telegraphs and railways were intercepted right across Europe, the main facts oozed out. An embargo had been laid on all the shipping in every port from the Baltic to Ostend; the fleets of the two great Powers had moved out, and it was supposed were assembled in the great northern harbor, and troops were hurrying on board all the steamers detained in these places, most of which were British vessels. It was clear that invasion was intended. Even then we might have been saved, if the fleet had been ready. The forts which guarded the flotilla were perhaps too strong for shipping

to attempt; but an iron-clad or two, handled as British
sailors knew how to use them, might have destroyed or
damaged a part of the transports, and delayed the expe-
dition, giving us what we wanted, time. But then the
best part of the fleet had been decoyed down to the
Dardanelles, and what remained of the Channel squadron
was looking after Fenian fillibusters off the west of Ireland; so it was ten days before the fleet was got together,
and by that time it was plain the enemy's preparations
were too far advanced to be stopped by a *coup-de-main.*
Information, which came chiefly through Italy, came
slowly, and was more or less vague and uncertain; but
this much was known, that at least a couple of hundred
thousand men were embarked or ready to be put on
board ships, and that the flotilla was guarded by more
iron-clads than we could then muster. I suppose it was
the uncertainty as to the point the enemy would aim at
for landing, and the fear lest he should give us the go-
by, that kept the fleet for several days in the Downs, but
it was not until the Tuesday fortnight after the declaration of war that it weighed anchor and steamed away for
the North Sea. Of course you have read about the
Queen's visit to the fleet the day before, and how she
sailed round the ships in her yacht, and went on board
the flag-ship to take leave of the admiral; how, over-
come with emotion, she told him that the safety of the
country was committed to his keeping. You remember,
too, the gallant old officer's reply, and how all the ships'
yards were manned, and how lustily the tars cheered as
her Majesty was rowed off. The account was of course
telegraphed to London, and the high spirits of the fleet
infected the whole town. I was outside the Charing
Cross station when the Queen's special train from Dover
arrived, and from the cheering and shouting which
greeted her as she drove away, you might have supposed

we had already won a great victory. The journals which had gone in strongly for the army reduction carried out during the session, and had been nervous and desponding in tone during the past fortnight, suggesting all sorts of compromises as a way of getting out of the war, came out in a very jubilant form next morning. "Panic-stricken inquirers," they said, "ask now, where are the means of meeting the invasion? We reply that the invasion will never take place. A British fleet, manned by British sailors, whose courage and enthusiasm are reflected in the people of this country, is already on the way to meet the presumptuous foe. The issue of a contest between British ships and those of any other country, under anything like equal odds, can never be doubtful. England awaits with calm confidence the issue of the impending action.

Such were the words of the leading article, and so we all felt. It was on Tuesday, the 10th of August, that the fleet sailed from the Downs. It took with it a submarine cable to lay down as it advanced, so that continuous communication was kept up, and the papers were publishing special editions every few minutes with the latest news. This was the first time such a thing had been done, and the feat was accepted as a good omen. Whether it is true that the Admiralty made use of the cable to keep on sending contradictory orders, which took the command out of the admiral's hands, I can't say; but all that the admiral sent in return was a few messages of the briefest kind, which neither the Admiralty nor any one else could have made any use of. Such a ship had gone off reconnoitring; such another had rejoined—fleet was in latitude so and so. This went on till the Thursday morning. I had just come up to town by train as usual, and was walking to my office, when the newsboys began to cry, "New edition—

enemy's fleet in sight!" You may imagine the scene in London! Business still went on at the banks, for bills matured although the independence of the country was being fought out under our own eyes, so to say; and the speculators were active enough. But even with the people who were making and losing their fortunes, the interest in the fleet overcame everything else; men who went to pay in or draw out their money stopped to show the last bulletin to the cashier. As for the street, you could hardly get along for the crowd stopping to buy and read the papers; while at every house or office the members sat restlessly in the common room, as if to keep together for company, sending out some one of their number every few minutes to get the latest edition. At least this is what happened in our office; but to sit still was as impossible as to do anything, and most of us went out and wandered about among the crowd, under a sort of feeling that the news was got quicker at in this way. Bad as were the times coming, I think the sickening suspense of that day, and the shock which followed, was almost the worst that we underwent. It was about ten o'clock that the first telegram came; an hour later the wire announced that the admiral had signalled to form line of battle, and shortly afterwards that the order was given to bear down on the enemy and engage. At twelve came the announcement, " Fleet opened fire about three miles to leeward of us "—that is, the ship with the cable. So far all had been expectancy, then came the first token of calamity. " An iron-clad has been blown up "—" the enemy's torpedoes are doing great damage "—" the flagship is laid aboard the enemy "—" the flagship appears to be sinking "—" the vice-admiral has signalled "—there the cable became silent, and, as you know, we heard no more till two days afterwards. The solitary iron-clad which escaped the disaster steamed into Portsmouth.

Then the whole story came out—how our sailors, gallant as ever, had tried to close with the enemy; how the latter evaded the conflict at close quarters, and, sheering off, left behind them the fatal engines which sent our ships, one after the other, to the bottom; how all this happened almost in a few minutes. The Government, it appears, had received warnings of this invention; but to the nation this stunning blow was utterly unexpected. That Thursday I had to go home early for regimental drill, but it was impossible to remain doing nothing, so when that was over I went up to town again, and after waiting in expectation of news which never came, and missing the midnight train, I walked home. It was a hot, sultry night, and I did not arrive till near sunrise. The whole town was quite still—the lull before the storm; and as I let myself in with my latch-key, and went softly up-stairs to my room to avoid waking the sleeping household, I could not but contrast the peacefulness of the morning—no sound breaking the silence but the singing of the birds in the garden—with the passionate remorse and indignation that would break out with the day. Perhaps the inmates of the rooms were as wakeful as myself; but the house in its stillness was just as it used to be when I came home alone from balls or parties in the happy days gone by. Tired though I was, I could not sleep, so I went down to the river and had a swim; and, on returning, found the household was assembled for early breakfast. A sorrowful household it was, although the burden pressing on each was partly an unseen one. My father, doubting whether his firm could last through the day; my mother, her distress about my brother, now with his regiment on the coast, already exceeding that which she felt for the public misfortune, had come down, although hardly fit to leave her room. My sister Clara was worst of all, for she

could not but try to disguise her special interest in the
fleet; and though we had all guessed that her heart was
given to the young lieutenant in the flagship—the first
to go down—a love unclaimed could not be told, nor
could we express the sympathy we felt for the poor girl.
That breakfast, the last meal we ever had together, was
soon ended, and my father and I went up to town by an
early train, and got there just as the fatal announcement
of the loss of the fleet was telegraphed from Portsmouth.

The panic and excitement of that day—how the
funds went down to 35; the run upon the bank and its
stoppage; the fall of half the houses in the city; how
the Government issued a notification suspending specie
payment and the tendering of bills—this last precaution
too late for most firms, Carter & Co. among the number,
which stopped payment as soon as my father got to the
office; the call to arms, and the unanimous response of
the country—all this is history which I need not repeat.
You wish to hear about my own share in the business at
the time. Well, volunteering had increased immensely
from the day war was proclaimed, and our regiment went
up in a day or two from its usual strength of 600 to nearly 1000. But the stock of rifles was deficient. We were
promised a further supply in a few days, which, however, we never received; and while waiting for them the
regiment had to be divided into two parts, the recruits
drilling with the rifles in the morning, and we old hands
in the evening. The failures and stoppage of work on
this black Friday threw an immense number of young
men out of employment, and we recruited up to 1400
strong by the next day; but what was the use of all these
men without arms? On Saturday it was announced
that a lot of smooth-bore muskets in store at the tower
would be served out to regiments applying for them, and
a regular scramble took place among the volunteers for

them, and our people got hold of a couple of hundred. But you might almost as well have tried to learn rifle-drill with a broomstick as with old brown bess; besides there was no smooth-bore ammunition in the country. A national subscription was opened for the manufacture of rifles at Birmingham, which ran up to a couple of million in two days, but, like every thing else, this came too late. To return to the volunteers: camps had been formed a fortnight before at Dover, Brighton, Harwich, and other places, of regulars and militia, and the head-quarters of most of the volunteer regiments were attached to one or other of them, and the volunteers themselves used to go down for drill from day to day, as they could spare time, and on Friday an order went out that they should be permanently embodied; but the metropolitan volunteers were still kept about London as a sort of reserve, till it could be seen at what point the invasion would take place. We were all told off to brigades and divisions. Our brigade consisted of the 4th Royal Surrey Militia, the 1st Surrey Administrative Battalion, as it was called, at Clapham, the 7th Surrey Volunteers at Southwark, and ourselves; but only our battalion and the militia were quartered in the same place, and the whole brigade had merely two or three afternoons together at brigade exercise in Bushey Park before the march took place. Our brigadier belonged to a line regiment in Ireland, and did not join till the very morning the order came. Meanwhile, during the preliminary fortnight, the militia colonel commanded. But though we volunteers were busy with our drill and preparations, those of us, who, like myself, belonged to Government offices, had more than enough of office work to do, as you may suppose. The volunteer clerks were allowed to leave office at four o'clock, but the rest were kept hard at the desk far into the night. Orders to the lord-

lieutenants, to the magistrates, notifications, all the arrangements for cleaning out the work-houses for hos-
pitals—these and a hundred other things had to be
managed in our office, and there was as much bustle in-
doors as out.   Fortunate we were to be so busy—the
people to be pitied were those who had nothing to do.
And on Sunday (that was the 15th August) work went
on just as usual.   We had an early parade and drill, and
I went up to town by the nine o'clock train in my uniform, taking my rifle with me in case of accidents, and
luckily too, as it turned out, a Mackintosh overcoat.
When I got to Waterloo there were all sorts of rumors
afloat.   A fleet had been seen off the downs, and some
of the despatch boats which were hovering about the
coasts brought news that there was a large flotilla off
Harwich, but nothing could be seen from the shore, as
the weather was hazy.   The enemy's light ships had
taken and sunk all the fishing-boats they could catch, to
prevent the news of their whereabouts reaching us, but
a few escaped during the night, and reported that the
Inconstant frigate coming home from North America,
without any knowledge of what had taken place, had
sailed right into the enemy's fleet and been captured.
In town the troops were all getting ready for a move;
the guards in the Wellington Barracks were under arms,
and their baggage wagons packed and drawn up in the
Bird-cage Walk.   The usual guard at the Horse Guards
had been withdrawn, and orderlies and staff-officers were
going to and fro.   All this I saw on the way to my
office, where I worked away till twelve o'clock, and then
feeling hungry after my early breakfast, I went across
Parliament Street to my club to get some luncheon.
There were about half-a-dozen men in the coffee-room,
none of whom I knew; but in a minute or two, Danvers
of the Treasury entered in a tremendous hurry.   From

him I got the first bit of authentic news I had had that day. The enemy had landed in force near Harwich, and the metropolitan regiments were ordered down there to reinforce the troops already collected in that neighbourhood; his regiment was to parade at one o'clock, and he had come to get something to eat before starting. We bolted a hurried lunch, and were just leaving the club when a messenger from the Treasury came running into the hall.

"Oh, Mr. Danvers," said he, "I've come to look for you, sir; the secretary says that all the gentlemen are wanted at the office, and that you must please not one of you go with the regiments."

"The devil!" cried Danvers.

"Do you know if that order extends to all the public offices? I asked.

"I don't know," said the man, "but I believe it do. I know there's messengers gone round to all the clubs and luncheon-bars to look for the gentlemen; the secretary says it's quite impossible any one can be spared just now, there's so much work to do; there's orders just come to send off our records to Birmingham to-night."

I did not wait to condole with Danvers; but, just glancing up Whitehall to see if any of our messengers were in pursuit, I ran off as hard as I could for Westminster Bridge, and so to the Waterloo station.

The place had quite changed its aspect since the morning. The regular service of trains had ceased, and the station and approaches were full of troops, among them the Guards and artillery. Everything was very orderly; the men had piled arms, and were standing about in groups. There was no sign of high spirits or enthusiasm. Matters had become too serious. Every man's face reflected the general feeling that we had neglected the warnings given us, and that now the danger so long derided as impossible and absurd had really come and found us unprepared. But the soldiers, if grave, looked determined, like men who meant to do their duty whatever might happen. A train full of Guardsmen was just starting for Guildford. I was told it would stop at Surbiton, and, with several other volunteers, hurrying like myself to join our regiment, got a place in it. We did not arrive a moment too soon, for the regiment was marching from Kingston down to the station. The destination of our brigade was the east coast. Empty carriages were drawn up in the siding, and our regiment was to go first. A large crowd was assembled to see it off, including the recruits who had joined during the last fortnight, and who formed by far the largest part of our strength. They were to stay behind, and were certainly very much in the way already; for as all the officers and sergeants belonged to the active part, there was no one to keep discipline among them, and they came crowding around us, breaking the ranks and making it difficult to get into the train. Here I saw our new brigadier for the first time. He was a soldier-like man, and no doubt knew his duty, but he appeared new to volunteers, and did not seem to know how to deal with gentlemen privates. I wanted very much to run home and get my greatcoat and knapsack, which I had bought a few days ago, but feared to be left behind; a good-natured recruit volunteered to fetch them for me, but he had not returned before we started, and I began the campaign with a kit consisting of a mackintosh and a small pouch of tobacco.

It was a tremendous squeeze in the train; for, besides the ten men sitting down, there were three or four standing up in every compartment, and the afternoon was close and sultry, and there were so many stoppages on

the way that we took nearly an hour and a half crawling
up to Waterloo. It was between five and six in the
afternoon when we arrived there, and it was nearly seven
before we marched up to the Shoreditch station. The
whole place was filled up with stores and ammunition,
to be sent off to the East, so we piled arms in the street
and scattered about to get food and drink, of which
most of us stood in need, especially the latter, for some
were already feeling the worse for the heat and crush.
I was just stepping into a public-house with Travers,
when who should drive up but his pretty wife! Most
of our friends had paid their adieus at the Surbiton station, but she had driven up by the road in his brougham,
bringing their little boy to have a last look at papa.
She had also brought his knapsack and greatcoat, and,
what was still more acceptable, a basket containing
fowls, tongue, bread-and-butter, and biscuits, and a
couple of bottles of claret—which priceless luxuries they
insisted on my sharing.

Meanwhile the hours went on. The 4th Surrey Militia, which had marched all the way from Kingston, had
come up, as well as the other volunteer corps; the station had been partly cleared of the stores that encum-
bered it; some artillery, two militia regiments, and a
battalion of the line, had been despatched, and our turn
to start had come, and long lines of carriages were drawn
up ready for us; but still we remained in the street.
You may fancy the scene. There seemed to be as many
people as ever in London, and we could hardly move for
the crowds of spectators—fellows hawking fruits and
volunteers' comforts, newsboys, and so forth, to say nothing of the cabs and omnibuses; while orderlies and staff-
officers were constantly riding up with messages. A
good many of the militiamen, and some of our people,
too, had taken more than enough to drink; perhaps a

hot sun had told on empty stomachs; anyhow, they became very noisy. The din, dirt, and heat were indescribable. So the evening wore on, and all the information our officers could get from the brigadier, who appeared to be acting under another general, was, that orders had come to stand fast for the present. Gradually the street became quieter and cooler. The brigadier, who, by way of setting an example, had remained for some hours without leaving his saddle, had got a chair out of a shop, and sat nodding in it; most of the men were lying down or sitting on the pavement—some sleeping, some smoking. In vain had Travers begged his wife to go home. She declared that, having come so far, she would stay and see the last of us. The brougham had been sent away to a by-street, as it blocked up the road; so he sat on a doorstep, she by him on the knapsack. Little Arthur, who had been delighted at the bustle and the uniforms, and in high spirits, became at last very cross, and eventually cried himself to sleep in his father's arms, his golden hair and one little dimpled arm hanging over his shoulder. Thus went on the weary hours, till suddenly the assembly sounded, and we all started up. We were to return to Waterloo. The landing on the east was only a feint— so ran the rumor—the real attack was on the south. Anything seemed better than indecision and delay, and, tired though we were, the march back was gladly hailed. Mrs. Travers, who made us take the remains of the luncheon with us, we left to look for her carriage; little Arthur, who was awake again, but very good and quiet, in her arms.

We did not reach Waterloo till nearly midnight, and there was some delay in starting again. Several volunteer and militia regiments had arrived from the north; the station and all its approaches were jammed up with men, and trains were being despatched away as fast as they could be made up. All this time no news had reached us since the first announcement; but the excitement then aroused had now passed away under the influence of fatigue and want of sleep, and most of us dozed off as soon as we got under way. I did, at any rate, and was awoke by the train stopping at Leatherhead. There was an up-train returning to town, and some persons in it were bringing up news from the coast. We could not, from our part of the train, hear what they said, but the rumor was passed up from one carriage to another. The enemy had landed in force at Worthing. Their position had been attacked by the troops from the camp near Brighton, and the action would be renewed in the morning. The volunteers had behaved very well. This was all the information we could get. So, then, the invasion had come at last. It was clear, at any rate, from what was said, that the enemy had not been driven back yet, and we should be in time most likely to take a share in the defence.

It was sunrise when the train crawled into Dorking, for there had been numerous stoppages on the way; and here it was pulled up for a long time, and we were told to get out and stretch ourselves—an order gladly responded to, for we had been very closely packed all night. Most of us, too, took the opportunity to make an early breakfast off the food we had brought from Shoreditch. I had the remains of Mrs. Travers' fowl and some bread wrapped up in my waterproof, which I shared with one or two less provident comrades. We could see from our halting place that the line was blocked with trains beyond and behind. It must have been about eight o'clock when we got orders to take our seats again, and the train began to move slowly on towards Horsham. Horsham Junction was the point to be occupied—so

the rumor went; but about ten o'clock, when halting
at a small station a few miles short of it, the order came
to leave the train, and our brigade formed in column on
the highroad. Beyond us was some field-artillery; and
further on, so we were told by a staff-officer, another
brigade, which was to make up a division with ours.
After more delays the line began to move, but not for-
wards; our route was towards the north-west, and a sort
of suspicion of the state of affairs flashed across my
mind. Horsham was already occupied by the enemy's
advance-guard, and we were to fall back on Leith Common, and take up a position threatening his flank, should
he advance either to Guildford or Dorking. This was
soon confirmed by what the colonel was told by the
brigadier and passed down the ranks; and just now for
the first time, the boom of artillery came up on the light
south breeze. In about an hour the firing ceased.
What did it mean? We could not tell. Meanwhile
our march continued. The day was very close and sultry, and the clouds of dust stirred up by our feet almost
suffocated us. I had saved a soda-water bottleful of
yesterday's claret; but this went only a short way, for
there were many mouths to share it with, and the thirst
soon became as bad as ever. Several of the regiment
fell out from faintness, and we made frequent halts to
rest and let the stragglers come up. At last we reached
the top of Leith Hill. It is a striking spot, being the
highest spot in the south of England. The view from it
is splendid, and most lovely did the country look this
summer day, although the grass was brown from the
long drought. It was a great relief to get from the
dusty road on to the common, and at the top of the hill
there was a refreshing breeze. We could see now for
the first time, the whole of our division. Our own regiment did not muster more than 500, for it contained a

large number of Government office men who had been detained, like Danvers, for duty in town, and others were not much larger; but the militia regiment was very strong, and the whole division, I was told mustered nearly 5000 rank and file. We could see other troops also in extension of our division, and could count a couple of field-batteries of Royal Artillery, besides some heavy guns belonging to the volunteers, apparently drawn by cart horses. The cooler air, the sense of numbers, and the evident strength of the position we held, raised our spirits, which, I am not ashamed to say, had all the morning been depressed. It was not that we were not eager to close with the enemy, but that the counter-marching and halting ominously betokened a vacillation of purpose in those who had the guidance of affairs. Here in two days the invaders had got more than twenty miles inland, and nothing effectual had been done to stop them. And the ignorance in which we volunteers, from the colonel downwards, were kept of their movements, filled us with uneasiness. We could not but depict to ourselves the enemy as carrying out all the while firmly his well-considered scheme of attack, and contrasting it with our own uncertainty of purpose. The very silence with which his advance appeared to be conducted filled us with mysterious awe. Meanwhile the day wore on, and we became faint with hunger, for we had eaten nothing since daybreak. No provisions came up, and there were no signs of any commissariat officers. It seems that when we were at the Waterloo station a whole trainful of provisions was drawn up there, and our colonel proposed that one of the trucks should be taken off and attached to our trains, so that we might have some food at hand; but the officer in charge, an assistant-controller, I think they call him—this control department was a newfangled affair

2

which did us almost as much harm as the enemy in the long run—said his orders were to keep all the stores together, and that he couldn't issue any without authority from the head of his department. So we had to go without. Those who had tobacco smoked—indeed there is no solace like a pipe under such circumstances. The militia regiment, I heard afterwards, had two days' provisions in their haversacks; it was we volunteers who had no haversacks, and nothing to put in them. All this time, I should tell you, while we were lying on the grass with our arms piled, the General, with the brigadiers and staff, was riding about slowly from point to point of the edge of the common, looking out with his glass towards the south valley. Orderlies and staff-officers were constantly coming, and about three o'clock there arrived up a road that led towards Horsham a small body of lancers and a regiment of yeomanry, who had, it appears been out in advance, and now drew up a short way in front of us in column facing to the south. Whether they could see anything in their front I could not tell, for we were behind the crest of the hill ourselves, and so could not look into the valley below; but shortly afterwards the assembly sounded. Commanding officers were called out by the General, and received some brief instructions; and the column began to march again towards London, the militia this time coming last in our brigade. A rumor regarding the object of this counter-march soon spread through the ranks. The enemy was not going to attack us here, but was trying to turn the position on both sides, one column pointing to Reigate, the other to Aldershot; and so we must fall back and take up a position at Dorking. The line of the great chalk-range was to be defended. A large force was concentrating at Guildford, another at Reigate, and we should find supports at Dorking. The enemy would

be awaited in these positions. Such, so far as we privates could get at the facts, was to be the plan of opera-
tions. Down the hill, therefore, we marched. From
one or two points we could catch a brief sight of the
railway in the valley below running from Dorking to
Horsham. Men in red were working upon it here and
there. They were the Royal Engineers, some one said,
breaking up the line. On we marched. The dust seemed
worse than ever.

In one village through which we passed—I forget the
name now—there was a pump on the green. Here we
stopped and had a good drink; and passing by a large
farm, the farmer's wife and two or three of her maids
stood at the gate and handed us hunches of bread and
cheese out of some baskets. I got the share of a bit, but
the bottom of the baskets must soon have been reached.
Not a thing else was to be had till we got to Dorking
about six o'clock; indeed, most of the farmhouses appeared deserted already. On arriving there, we were
drawn up in the street, and just opposite was a baker's
shop. Our fellows asked leave, at first by twos and
threes, to go in and buy some loaves, but soon others
began to break off and crowd into the shop, and at last
a regular scramble took place. If there had been any
order preserved, and a regular distribution arranged,
they would, no doubt, have been steady enough, but
hunger makes men selfish: each man felt that his stopping behind would do no good—he would simply lose
his share; so it ended by almost the whole regiment
joining in the scrimmage, and the shop was cleared out
in a couple of minutes; while as for paying, you could
not get your hand into your pocket for the crush. The
colonel tried in vain to stop the row; some of the officers
were as bad as the men. Just then a staff officer rode
by; he could scarcely make way for the crowd, and was

pushed against rather rudely, and in a passion he called out to us to behave properly, like soldiers, and not like a parcel of roughs. "Oh, blow it, governor," says Dick Wake, " you arn't agoing to come between a poor cove and his grub." Wake was an articled attorney, and, as we used to say in those days, a cheeky young chap, although a good-natured fellow enough. At this speech, which was followed by some more remarks of the sort from those about him, the staff officer became angrier still. " Orderly," cried he to the lancer riding behind him, " take that man to the provost-marshal. As for you, sir," he said, turning to our colonel, who sat on his horse, silent with astonishment, " if you don't want some of your men shot before their time, you and your precious officers had better keep this rabble in a little better order:" and poor Dick, who looked crest-fallen enough, would certainly have been led off at the tail of the sergeant's horse, if the brigadier had not come up and arranged matters, and marched us off to the hill beyond the town. This incident made us both angry and crest-fallen. We were annoyed at being so roughly spoken to: at the same time, we felt we had deserved it, and were ashamed of the misconduct. Then, too, we had lost confidence in our colonel, after the poor figure he cut in the affair. He was a good fellow, the colonel, and showed himself a brave one next day ; but he aimed too much at being popular, and didn't understand a bit how to command.

To resume :—We had scarcely reached the hill above the town, which we were told was to be our bivouac for the night, when the welcome news came that a food-train had arrived at the station ; but there were no carts to bring the things up, so a fatigue-party went down and carried back a supply to us in their arms—loaves, a barrel of rum, packets of tea, and joints of meat—abundance for all; but there was not a kettle or a cooking-pot in the regiment, and we could not eat the meat raw. The colonel and officers were no better off. They had arranged to have a regular mess, with crockery, steward, and all complete, but the establishment never turned up, and what had become of it no one knew. Some of us were sent back into the town to see what we could procure in the way of cooking utensils. We found the street full of artillery, baggage-wagons, and mounted officers, and volunteers shopping like ourselves; and all the houses appeared to be occupied by troops. We succeeded in getting a few kettles and saucepans, and I obtained for myself a leather bag, with a strap to go over the shoulder, which proved very handy afterwards; and thus laden, we trudged back to our camp on the hill, filling the kettles with dirty water from a little stream which runs between the hill and the town, for there was none to be had above. It was nearly a couple of miles each way; and, exhausted as we were with marching and want of rest, we were almost too tired to eat. The cooking was of the roughest, as you may suppose; all we could do was to cut off slices of the meat and boil them in the saucepans, using our fingers for forks. The tea, however, was very refreshing; and, thirsty as we were, we drank it by the gallon. Just before it grew dark, the brigade-major came round, and, with the adjutant, showed our colonel how to set a picket in advance of our line, a little way down the face of the hill. It was not necessary to place one, I suppose, because the town in our front was still occupied with troops; but, no doubt, the practice would be useful. We had also a quarter-guard, and a line of sentries in front and rear of our line, communicating with those of the regiments on our flanks. Firewood was plentiful, for the hill was covered with beautiful wood; but it took some time to collect it, for we had nothing but our pocket-knives to cut down the branches with.

So we lay down to sleep. My company had no duty, and we had the night undisturbed to ourselves; but, tired though I was, the excitement and the novelty of the situation made sleep difficult. And although the night was still and warm, and we were sheltered by the woods, I soon found it chilly with no better covering than my thin dust-coat, the more so as my clothes, saturated with perspiration during the day, had never dried; and before daylight, I woke from a short nap, shivering with cold, and was glad to get warm with others by a fire. I then noticed that the opposite hills on the south were dotted with fires; and we thought at first they must belong to the enemy, but we were told that the ground up there was still held by a strong rear-guard of regulars, and that there need be no fear of a surprise.

At the first sign of dawn, the bugles of the regiments sounded the *reveillé*, and we were ordered to fall in, and the roll was called. About twenty men were absent, who had fallen out sick the day before; they had been sent up to London by train during the night, I believe. After standing in column for about half an hour, the brigade-major came down with orders to pile arms and stand easy; and perhaps half an hour afterwards we were told to get breakfast as quickly as possible, and to cook a day's food at the same time. This operation was managed pretty much in the same way as the evening before, except that we had our cooking-pots and kettles ready.

Meantime, there was leisure to look around, and from where we stood there was a commanding view of one of the most beautiful scenes in England. Our regiment was drawn up on the extremity of the ridge which runs from Guildford to Dorking. This is indeed merely a part of the great chalk-range which extends from beyond Aldershot east to the Medway; but there is a gap in the ridge just here, where the little stream that runs past Dorking turns suddenly to the north, to find its way to the Thames. We stood on the slope of the hill, as it trends down eastward toward this gap, and had passed our bivouac in what appeared to be a gentleman's park. A little way above us, and to our right, was a very fine country seat to which the park was attached, now occupied by the headquarters of our division. From this house the hill sloped steeply down southward to the valley below, which runs nearly east and west parallel to the ridge, and carries the railway and the road from Guildford to Reigate, and in which valley, immediately in front of the chateau, and perhaps a mile and a half distant from it, was the little town of Dorking, nestled in the trees, and rising up the foot of the slopes on the other side of the valley, which stretched away to Leith Common, the scene of yesterday's march. Thus the main part of the town of Dorking was on our right front, but the suburbs stretched away eastward nearly to our proper front, culminating in a small railway station, from which the grassy slopes of the park rose up dotted with shrubs and trees to where we were standing. Round this railway station was a cluster of villas and one or two mills, of whose gardens we thus had a bird's-eye view, their little ornamental ponds glistening like looking-glasses in the morning sun. Immediately on our left the park sloped steeply down to the gap before mentioned, through which ran the little stream, as well as the railway from Epsom to Brighton, nearly due north and south, meeting the Guildford and Reigate line at right angles. Close to the point of intersection and the little station already mentioned, was the station of the former line where we had stopped the day before. Beyond the gap on the east (our left), and in continuation of our ridge, rose the chalk-hill again. The shoulder of this ridge overlooking the gap is called Box Hill, from the shrubbery of box-wood with which it was covered. Its sides were very steep, and the top of the ridge was covered with troops. The natural strength of our position was manifest at a glance; a high grassy ridge, steep to the south, with a stream in front, and but little cover up the sides. It seemed made for a battle-field. The weak point was the gap; the ground at the junction of the railways and the roads immediately at the entrance of the gap formed a little valley, dotted, as I have said, with buildings and gardens. This, in one sense, was the key of the position; for although it would not be tenable while we held the ridge commanding it, the enemy, by carrying this point and advancing through the gap, would cut our line in two. But you must not suppose I scanned the ground thus critically at the time. Anybody, indeed, might have been struck with the natural advantages of our position; but what, as I remember, most impressed me, was the peaceful beauty of the scene —the little town, with the outline of the houses obscured by a blue mist; the massive crispness of the foliage, the outlines of the great trees, lighted up by the sun, and relieved by a deep blue shade. So thick was the timber here, rising up the southern slopes of the valley, that it looked almost as if it might have been a primeval forest. The quiet of the scene was the more impressive because contrasted in the mind with the scenes we expected to follow; and I can remember, as if it were yesterday, the sensation of bitter regret that it should now be too late to avert this coming desecration of our country, which might so easily have been prevented. A little firmness, a little prevision on the part of our rulers, even a little common-sense, and this great calamity would have been rendered utterly impossible. Too late, alas! We were like the foolish virgins in the parable.

But you must not suppose the scene immediately around was gloomy: the camp was brisk and bustling enough. We had got over the stress of weariness; our stomachs were full; we felt a natural enthusiasm at the prospect of having so soon to take a part as the real defenders of the country, and we were inspirited at the sight of the large force that was now assembled. Along the slope which trended off to the rear of our ridge, troops came marching up—volunteers, militia, cavalry, and guns; these, I heard, had come down from the north as far as Leatherhead the night before, and had marched over at daybreak. Long trains, too, began to arrive by the rail through the gap, one after the other, containing militia and volunteers, who moved up to the ridge to the right and left, and took up their position, massed for the most part on the slopes which ran up from, and in rear of, where we stood. We now formed part of an army corps, we were told, consisting of three divisions, but what regiments composed the other two divisions, I never heard. All this movement we could distinctly see from our position, for we had hurried over our breakfast expecting every minute that the battle would begin, and now stood or sat about on the ground near our piled arms. Early in the morning, too, we saw a very long train come along the valley from the direction of Guildford, full of redcoats. It halted at the little station at our feet, and the troops alighted. We could soon make out their bear-skins. They were the Guards, coming to reinforce this part of the line. Leaving a detachment of skirmishers to hold the line of the railway embankment, the main body marched up with a springy step and with the band playing, and drew up across the gap on our

*2

left, in prolongation of our line. There appeared to be three battalions of them, for they formed up in that number of columns at short intervals.

Shortly after this, I was sent over to Box Hill with a message from our colonel to the colonel of a volunteer regiment stationed there, to know whether an ambulance-cart was obtainable, as it was reported this regiment was well supplied with carriage, whereas we were without any: my mission, however, was futile. Crossing the valley, I found a scene of great confusion at the railway station. Trains were still coming in with stores, ammunition, guns, and appliances of all sorts, which were being unloaded as fast as possible; but there were scarcely any means of getting the things off. There were plenty of wagons of all sorts, but hardly any horses to draw them, and the whole place was blocked up; while, to add to the confusion, a regular exodus had taken place of the people from the town, who had been warned that it was likely to be the scene of fighting. Ladies and women of all sorts and ages, and children, some with bundles, some empty-handed, were seeking places in the train, but there appeared no one on the spot authorised to grant them; and these poor creatures were pushing their way up and down, vainly asking for information and permission to get away.

In the crowd I observed our surgeon, who likewise was in search of an ambulance of some sort: his whole professional apparatus, he said, consisted of a case of instruments. Also in the crowd I stumbled upon Wood, Travers's old coachman. He had been sent down by his mistress to Guildford, because it was supposed our regiment had gone there, riding the horse, and laden with a supply of things—food, blankets, and of course, a letter. He had also brought my knapsack; but at Guildford the horse was pressed for artillery work, and a receipt for it

given him in exchange, so he had been obliged to leave
all the heavy packages there, including my knapsack;
but the faithful old man had brought on as many things
as he could carry, and hearing that we should be found
in this part, had walked over thus laden from Guildford.
He said that place was crowded with troops, and that
the heights were lined with them the whole way between
the two towns; also, that some trains with wounded had
passed up from the coast in the night, through Guildford.
I led him off to where our regiment was, relieving the
old man from part of the load he was staggering under.
The food sent was not now so much needed, but the
plates, knives, &c., and drinking vessels, promised to be
handy—and Travers, you may be sure, was delighted to
get his letter; while a couple of newspapers the old man
had brought were eagerly competed for by all, even at
this critical moment, for we had heard no authentic news
since we left London on Sunday. And even at this distance of time, although I only glanced down the paper,
I can remember almost the very words I read there.
They were both copies of the same paper—the first, published on Sunday evening, when the news had arrived of
the successful landing at three points, was written in a
tone of despair. The country must confess that it had
been taken by surprise. The conqueror would be satis-
fied with the humiliation inflicted by a peace dictated on
our own shores; it was the clear duty of the Government
to accept the best terms obtainable, and to avoid further
bloodshed and disaster, and avert the fall of our totter-
ing mercantile credit. The next morning's issue was in
quite a different tone. Apparently the enemy had received a check, for we were here exhorted to resistance.
An impregnable position was to be taken up along the
Downs, a force was concentrating there far outnumber-
ing the rash invaders, who, with an invincible line before

them, and the sea behind, had no choice between destruction or surrender. Let there be no pusillanimous talk of negotiation, the fight must be fought out; and there could be but one issue. England, expectant but calm, awaited with confidence the result of the attack on its unconquerable volunteers. The writing appeared to me eloquent, but rather inconsistent. The same paper said the Government had sent off 500 workmen from Woolwich, to open a branch arsenal at Birmingham.

All this time we had nothing to do, except to change our position, which we did every few minutes, now moving up the hill farther to our right, now taking ground lower down to our left, as one order after another was brought down the line; but the staff-officers were galloping about perpetually with orders, while the rumble of the artillery as they moved about from one part of the field to another went on almost incessantly. At last the whole line stood to arms, the bands struck up, and the general commanding our army corps came riding down with his staff. We had seen him several times before, as we had been moving frequently about the position during the morning; but he now made a sort of formal inspection. He was a tall, thin man, with long, light hair, very well mounted, and as he sat on his horse with an erect seat, and came prancing down the line, at a little distance he looked as if he might be five-and-twenty; but I believe he had served more than fifty years, and had been made a peer for services performed when quite an old man. I remember that he had more decorations than there was room for on the breast of his coat, and wore them suspended like a necklace round his neck. Like all the other generals, he was dressed in blue, with a cocked-hat and feathers—a bad plan, I thought, for it made them very conspicuous. The general halted before our battalion, and after looking at us a while, made a short address: We had a post of honor next her Majesty's Guards, and would show ourselves worthy of it, and of the name of Englishmen. It did not need, he said, to be a general to see the strength of our position; it was impregnable, if properly held. Let us wait till the enemy was well pounded, and then the word would be given to go at him. Above everything, we must be steady. He then shook hands with our colonel, we gave him a cheer, and he rode on to where the Guards were drawn up.

Now then, we thought, the battle will begin. But still there were no signs of the enemy; and the air, though hot and sultry, began to be very hazy, so that you could scarcely see the town below, and the hills opposite were merely a confused blur, to which no features could be distinctly made out. After a while, the tension of feeling which followed the general's address relaxed, and we began to feel less as if everything depended on keeping our rifles firmly grasped: we were told to pile arms again, and got leave to go down by tens and twenties to the stream below to drink. This stream, and all the hedges and banks on our side of it, were held by our skirmishers, but the town had been abandoned. The position appeared an excellent one, except that the enemy, when they came, would have almost better cover than our men. While I was down at the brook, a column emerged from the town, making for our position. We thought for a moment it was the enemy, and you could not make out the color of the uniforms for the dust; but it turned out to be our rear-guard, falling back from the opposite hills which they had occupied the previous night. One battalion of rifles halted for a few minutes at the stream to let the men drink, and I had a minute's talk with a couple of the officers. They had formed part of the force which had attacked the enemy on their first landing. They had it all their own way,

they said, at first, and could have beaten the enemy back
easily if they had been properly supported; but the
whole thing was mismanaged. The volunteers came on
very pluckily, they said, but they got into confusion,
and so did the militia, and the attack failed with serious
loss. It was the wounded of this force which had passed
through Guildford in the night. The officers asked us
eagerly about the arrangements for the battle, and when
we said that the Guards were the only regular troops in
this part of the field, shook their heads ominously.

While we were talking, a third officer came up; he
was a dark man, with a smooth face and a curious, ex-
cited manner. "You are volunteers, I suppose," he said,
quickly, his eye flashing the while. "Well, now, look
here; mind, I don't want to hurt your feelings, or to say
anything unpleasant, but I'll tell you what: if all you
gentlemen were just to go back, and leave us to fight it
out alone, it would be a devilish good thing. We could
do it a precious deal better without you, I assure you.
We don't want your help, I can tell you. We would
much rather be left alone, I assure you. Mind, I don't
want to say anything rude, but that's a fact." Having
blurted out this passionately, he strode away before any
one could reply, or the other officers could stop him.
They apologized for his rudeness, saying that his brother, also in the regiment, had been killed on Sunday,
and that this, and the sun, and marching, had affected
his head. The officers told us that the enemy's ad-
vanced-guard was close behind, but that he had apparently been waiting for reinforcements, and would prob-
ably not attack in force until noon. It was, however,
nearly three o'clock before the battle began. We had
almost worn out the feeling of expectancy. For twelve
hours had we been waiting for the coming struggle, till
at last it seemed almost as if the invasion were but a bad

dream, and the enemy, as yet unseen by us, had no real existence. So far, things had not been very different, but for the numbers and for what we had been told, from a Volunteer review on Brighton Downs. I remember that these thoughts were passing through my mind as we lay down in groups on the grass, some smoking, some nibbling at their bread, some even asleep, when the listless state we had fallen into was suddenly disturbed by a gunshot fired from the top of the hill on our right, close by the big house. It was the first time I had ever heard a shotted gun fired, and although it is fifty years ago, the angry whistle of the shot, as it left the gun, is in my ears now. The sound was soon to become common enough. We all jumped up at the report, and fell in almost without the word being given, grasping our rifles tightly, and the leading files peering forward to look for the approaching enemy. This gun was apparently the signal to begin, for now our batteries opened fire all along the line. What they were firing at I could not see, and I am sure the gunners could not see much themselves. I have told you what a haze had come over the air since the morning, and now the smoke from the guns settled like a pall over the hill, and soon we could see little but the men in our ranks, and the outline of some gunners in the battery drawn up next us on the slope on our right. This firing went on, I should think, for nearly a couple of hours, and still there was no reply. We could see the gunners—it was a troop of horse-artillery—working away like fury, ramming, loading, and running up with cartridges, the officer in command riding slowly up and down just behind his guns, and peering out with his field-glass into the mist. Once or twice they ceased firing to let their smoke clear away, but this did not do much good. For nearly two hours did this go on, and not a shot came in reply. If a battle is like

this, said Dick Wake, who was my next-hand file, it's
mild work, to say the least. The words were hardly
uttered when a rattle of musketry was heard in front;
our skirmishers were at it, and very soon the bullets
began to sing over our heads, and some struck the
ground at our feet. Up to this time we had been in
column; we were now deployed into line on the ground
assigned to us. From the valley or gap on our left there
ran a lane right up the hill almost due west, or along
our front. This lane had a thick bank about four feet
high, and the greater part of the regiment was drawn
up behind it; but a little way up the hill the lane
trended back out of the line, so the right of the regiment
here left it and occupied the open grass-land of the park.
The bank had been cut away at this point to admit of
our going in and out. We had been told in the morning to cut down the bushes on the top of the bank, so as
to make the space clear-for firing over, but we had no
tools to work with; however, a party of sappers had
come down and finished the job. My company was on
the right, and was thus beyond the shelter of the friendly
bank. On our right, again, was the battery of artillery
already mentioned; then came a battalion of the line,
then more guns, then a great mass of militia and volunteers and a few line up to the big house. At least this
was the order before the firing began; after that I do
not know what changes took place.

And now the enemy's artillery began to open; where
their guns were posted we could not see, but we began
to hear the rush of the shells over our heads, and the
bang as they burst just beyond. And now what took
place I can really hardly tell you. Sometimes when I
try and recall the scene, it seems as if it lasted for only
a few minutes; yet, I know, as we lay on the ground, I
thought the hours would never pass away, as we watched

the gunners still plying their task, firing at the invisible enemy, never stopping for a moment except when now and again a dull blow would be heard and a man fall down, then three or four of his comrades would carry him to the rear. The captain no longer rode up and down; what had become of him I do not know. Two of the guns ceased firing for a time; they had got injured in some way, and up rode an artillery general. I think I see him now, a very handsome man, with straight features and a dark moustache, his breast covered with medals. He appeared in a great rage at the guns stopping fire.

"Who commands this battery?" he cried.

"I do, Sir Henry," said an officer, riding forward, whom I had not noticed before.

The group is before me at this moment, standing out clear against the background of smoke, Sir Henry erect on his splendid charger, his flashing eye, his left arm pointing towards the enemy to enforce something he was going to say, the young officer reining in his horse just beside him, and saluting with his right hand raised to his busby. This, for a moment, then a dull thud, and both horses and riders are prostrate on the ground. A round shot had struck all four at the saddle line. Some of the gunners ran up to help, but neither officer could have lived many minutes. This was not the first I saw killed. Some time before this, almost immediately on the enemy's artillery opening, as we were lying, I heard something like the sound of steel striking steel, and at the same moment Dick Wake, who was next me in the ranks, leaning on his elbows, sank forward on his face. I looked round and saw what had happened; a shot fired at a high elevation, passing over his head, had struck the ground behind, nearly cutting his thigh off. It must have been the ball striking his sheathed bayonet which made the noise. Three of us carried the poor fellow to the rear with difficulty, for the shattered limb; but he was nearly dead from loss of blood when we got to the doctor, who was waiting in a sheltered hollow about two hundred yards in rear, with two other doctors in plain clothes, who had come up to help. We deposited our burden and returned to the front. Poor Wake was sensible when we left him, but apparently too shaken by the shock to be able to speak. Wood was there, helping the doctors. I paid more visits to the rear, of the same sort, before the evening was over.

All this time we were lying there to be fired at without returning a shot, for our skirmishers were holding the line of walls and enclosures below. However, the bank protected most of us, and the brigadier now ordered our right company, which was in the open, to get behind it also; and there we lay about four deep, the shells crashing and bullets whistling over our heads, but hardly a man being touched. Our colonel was, indeed, the only one exposed, for he rode up and down the lane at a foot-pace, as steady as a rock; but he made the major and adjutant dismount, and take shelter behind the hedge, holding their horses. We were all pleased to see him so cool, and it restored our confidence in him, which had been shaken yesterday.

The time seemed interminable while we lay thus inactive. We could not, of course, help peering over the bank to try and see what was going on; but there was nothing to be made out, for now a tremendous thunderstorm, which had been gathering all day, burst on us, and a torrent of almost blinding rain came down, which obscured the view even more than the smoke, while the crashing of the thunder and the glare of the lightning could be heard and seen even above the roar and flashing of the artillery. Once the mist lifted, and I saw for a minute an attack on Box Hill, on the other side of the gap on our left. It was like the scene at a theatre—a curtain of smoke all round and a clear gap in the centre, with a sudden gleam of evening sunshine lighting it up. The steep, smooth slope of the hill was crowded with the dark-blue figures of the enemy, whom I now saw for the first time—an irregular outline in front, but very solid in rear: the whole body was moving forward by fits and starts, the men firing and advancing, the officers waving their swords, the columns closing up and gradually making way. Our people were almost concealed by the bushes at the top, whence the smoke and their fire could be seen proceeding: presently, from these bushes on the crest came out a red line, and dashed down the brow of the hill, a flame of fire belching out from the front as it advanced. The enemy hesitated, gave way, and finally ran back in a confused crowd down the hill. Then the mist covered the scene, but the glimpse of this splendid charge was inspiriting, and I hoped we should show the same coolness when it came to our turn. It was about this time that our skirmishers fell back, a good many wounded, some limping along by themselves, others helped. The main body retired in very fair order, halting to turn round and fire; we could see a mounted officer of the guards riding up and down encouraging them to be steady. Now came our turn. For a few minutes we saw nothing, but a rattle of bullets came through the rain and mist, mostly, however, passing over the bank. We began to fire in reply, stepping up against the bank to fire, and stooping down to load; but our brigade-major rode up with an order, and the word was passed through the men to reserve our fire. In a very few moments, it must have been, that, when ordered to stand, we could see the helmet-spikes, and then the figures of the skirmishers, as they came on: a lot of them there appeared to be, five or six deep, I should say, but in loose order, each man stopping to aim and fire, and then coming forward a little. Just then the brigadier clattered on horseback up the lane. " Now, then, gentlemen, give it to them hot," he cried; and fire away we did, as fast as ever we were able. A perfect storm of bullets seemed to be flying about us too, and I thought each moment must be the last; escape seemed impossible; but I saw no one fall, for I was too busy, and so were we all, to look to the right or left, but loaded and fired as fast as I could. How long this went on I know not—it could not have been long; neither side could have lasted many minutes under such a fire; but it ended by the enemy gradually falling back, and as soon as we saw this, we raised a tremendous shout, and some of us jumped up on the bank to give them our parting shots. Suddenly, the order was passed down the line to cease firing, and we soon discovered the cause; a battalion of the Guards was charging obliquely across from our left across our front. It was, I expect, their flank attack, as much as our fire, which had turned back the enemy; and it was a splendid sight to see their steady line, as they advanced slowly across the smooth lawn below us, firing as they went, but as steady as if on parade. We felt a great elation at this moment; it seemed as if the battle was won. Just then somebody called out to look to the wounded, and for the first time I turned to glance down the rank along the lane. Then I saw that we had not beaten back the attack without loss. Immediately before me lay Lawford of my office, dead on his back from a bullet through his forehead, his hand still grasping his rifle. At every step was some friend or acquaintance killed or wounded, and a few paces down the lane I found Travers, sitting with his back against the bank. A ball had gone through his lungs, and blood was

coming from his mouth. I was lifting him, but the
cry of agony he gave stopped me. I then saw that this
was not his only wound; his thigh was smashed by
a bullet (which must have struck him when standing on
the bank), and the blood streaming down mixed in a
muddy puddle with the rain-water under him. Still he
could not be left here, so, lifting him up as well as I
could, I carried him through the gate which led out of
the lane at the back to where our camp hospital was in
the rear. The movement must have caused him awful
agony, for I could not support the broken thigh, and he
could not restrain his groans, brave fellow though he
was; but how I carried him at all I cannot make out, for
he was a much bigger man than myself; but I had not
gone far, one of a stream of our fellows, all on the same
errand, when a bandsman and Wood met me, bringing a
hurdle as a stretcher, and on this we placed him. Wood
had just time to tell me that he had got a cart down in
the hollow, and would endeavour to take off his master
at once to Kingston, when a staff-officer rode up to call
us to the ranks. "You really must not straggle in this
way, gentlemen," he said; "pray keep your ranks."
"But we can't leave our wounded to be trodden down
and die," cried one of our fellows. "Beat off the enemy
first, sir, he replied. "Gentlemen, do, pray, join your
regiments, or we shall be a regular mob." And, no
doubt he did not speak too soon; for besides our fellows
straggling to the rear, lots of volunteers from the regiments in reserve were running forward to help, till the
whole ground was dotted with groups of men.

I hastened back to my post, but I had just time to
notice that all the ground in our rear was occupied by a
thick mass of troops, much more numerous than in the
morning, and a column was moving down to the left of
our line, to the ground now held by the Guards. All

this time, although the musketry had slackened, the artillery fire seemed heavier than ever ; the shells screamed
overhead or burst around ; and I confess to feeling quite
a relief at getting back to the friendly shelter of the
lane.   Looking over the bank, I noticed for the first time
the frightful execution our fire had created.   The space
in front was thickly strewed with dead or badly wounded,
and beyond the bodies of the fallen enemy could just be
seen—for it was now getting dusk—the bearskins and
red coats of our own gallant Guards scattered over the
slope, and marking the line of their victorious advance.
But hardly a minute could have passed in thus looking
over the field, when our brigade-major came moving up
the lane on foot (I suppose his horse had been shot),
crying, " Stand to your arms, Volunteers ! they're coming on again ; " and we found ourselves a second time engaged in a hot musketry fire.   How long it went on I
cannot now remember, but we could distinguish clearly
the thick line of skirmishers, about sixty paces off, and
mounted officers among them ; and we seemed to be
keeping them well in check, for they were quite exposed
to our fire, while we were protected nearly up to our
shoulders, when—I know not how—I became sensible
that something had gone wrong.   " We are taken in
flank ! " called out some one ; and looking along the left,
sure enough there were dark figures jumping over the
bank into the lane and firing up along our line.   The
volunteers in reserve, who had come down to take the
place of the Guards, must have given way at this point ;
the enemy's skirmishers had got through our line, and
turned our left flank.   How the next move came about I
cannot recollect, or whether it was without orders, but
in a short time we found ourselves out of the lane and
drawn up in a straggling line about thirty yards in rear
of it—at our end, that is, the other flank had fallen back

a good deal more—and the enemy were lining the hedge, and numbers of them passing over and forming up on our side. Beyond our left a confused mass were retreating, firing as they went, followed by the advancing line of the enemy. We stood in this way for a short space, firing at random as fast as we could. Our colonel and major must have been shot, for there was no one to give an order, when somebody on horseback called out from behind—I think it must have been the brigadier—"Now, then, Volunteers! give a British cheer, and go at them—charge!" and, with a shout, we rushed at the enemy. Some ran, some of them stopped to meet us, and for a moment it was a real hand-to-hand fight. I felt a sharp sting in my leg, as I drove my bayonet right through the man in front of me. I confess I shut my eyes, for I just got a glimpse of the poor wretch as he fell back, his eyes starting out of his head, and, savage though we were, the sight was almost too horrible to look at. But the struggle was over in a second, and we had cleared the ground again right up to the rear hedge of the lane. Had we gone on, I believe we might have recovered the lane too, but we were now all out of order; there was no one to say what to do; the enemy began to line the hedge and open fire; and they were streaming past our left; and how it came about I know not, but we found ourselves falling back towards our right rear, scarce any semblance of a line remaining, and the volunteers who had given way on our left mixed up with us, and adding to the confusion. It was now nearly dark. On the slopes which we were retreating to was a large mass of reserves drawn up in columns. Some of the leading files of these, mistaking us for the enemy, began firing at us; our fellows, crying out to them to stop, ran towards their ranks, and in a few moments the whole slope of the hill became a scene of confusion that I cannot attempt to

describe, regiments and detachments mixed up in hopeless disorder. Most of us, I believe, turned towards the
enemy and fired away our few remaining cartridges; but
it was too late to take aim, fortunately for us, or the guns
which the enemy had brought up through the gap, and
were firing point-blank, would have done more damage.
As it was, we could see little more than the bright
flashes of their fire. In our confusion we had jammed up
a line regiment immediately behind us, and its colonel and
some staff officers were in vain trying to make a passage
for it, and their shouts to us to march to the rear and
clear a road could be heard above the roar of the guns,
and the confused babel of sound. At last a mounted
officer pushed his way through, followed by a company
in sections, the men brushing past with firm-set faces, as
if on a desperate task; and the battalion, when it got
clear, appear to deploy and advance down the slope.
I have also a dim recollection of seeing the Life Guards
trot past the front, and push on towards the town—a
last desperate attempt to save the day—before we left
the field. Our adjutant, who had got separated from
our flank of the regiment in the confusion, now came up,
and managed to lead us, or at any rate some of us, up
to the crest of the hill in the rear, to re-form, as he said;
but there we met a vast crowd of volunteers, militia, and
wagons, all hurrying rearward from the direction of
the big house, and we were borne in the stream for a
mile at least before it was possible to stop. At last the
adjutant led us to an open space a little off the line of
fugitives, and there we reformed the remains of the companies. Telling us to halt, he rode off to try and obtain
orders, and find out where the rest of our brigade was.
From this point, a spur of high ground running off from
the main plateau, we looked down through the dim twi-
light into the battle-field below. Artillery fire was still

going on. We could see the flashes from the guns on both sides, and now and then a stray shell came screaming up and burst near us, but we were beyond the sound of musketry. This halt first gave time to think about what had happened. The long day of expectancy had been succeeded by the excitement of battle; and when each minute may be your last, you do not think much about other people, nor when you are facing another man with a rifle have you time to consider whether he or you are the invader, or that you are fighting for your home and hearths. All fighting is pretty much alike, I suspect, as to sentiment, when once it begins. But now we had time for reflection; and although we did not yet quite undestand how far the day had gone against us, an uneasy feeling of self-condemnation must have come up in the minds of most of us; while, above all, we now began to realise what the loss of this battle meant to the country. Then, too, we knew not of what had become of all our wounded comrades. Reaction, too, set in after the fatigue and excitement. For myself, I had found out for the first time that besides the bayonet-wound in my leg, a bullet had gone through my left arm, just below the shoulder, and outside the bone. I remember feeling something like a blow just when we lost the lane, but the wound passed unnoticed until now, when the bleeding had stopped and the shirt was sticking to the wound.

This half-hour seemed an age, and while we stood on this knoll the endless tramp of men and rumbling of carts along the downs beside us told their own tale. The whole army was falling back. At last we could discern the adjutant riding up to us out of the dark. The army was to retreat, and take up a position on Epsom Downs, he said; we should join in the march, and try and find our brigade in the morning; and so we turned into the throng again, and made our way on as

3

best we could. A few scraps of news he gave us as he
rode alongside of our leading section; the army held its
position well for a time, but the enemy had at last
broken through the line between us and Guildford, as
well as in our front, and had poured his men through the
point gained, throwing the line into confusion, and the
first army corps near Guildford were also falling back to
avoid being outflanked. The regular troops were holding
the rear; we were to push on as fast as possible to get
out of their way, and allow them to make an orderly retreat in the morning. The gallant old lord commanding
our corps had been badly wounded early in the day, he
heard, and carried off the field. The Guards had suf-
fered dreadfully; the household cavalry had ridden
down the cuirassiers, but had got into broken ground
and been awfully cut up. Such was the scraps of news
passed down our weary column. What had become of
our wounded no one knew, and no one liked to ask. So
we trudged on. It must have been midnight when we
reached Leatherhead. Here we left the open ground
and took to the road, and the block became greater. We
pushed our way painfully along; several trains passed
slowly ahead along the railway by the roadside, containing the wounded, we supposed—such of them, at least, as
were lucky enough to be picked up. It was daylight
when we got to Epsom. The night had been bright and
clear after the storm, with a cool air, which, blowing
through my soaking clothes, chilled me to the bone.
My wounded leg was stiff and sore, and I was ready to
drop with exhaustion and hunger. Nor were my comrades in much better case; we had eaten nothing since
breakfast the day before, and the bread we had put by
been washed away by the storm—only a little pulp
had remained at the bottom of my bag. The tobacco
was all too wet to smoke. In this plight we were creep-

ing along, when the adjutant guided us into a field by
the roadside to rest awhile, and we lay down exhausted
on the sloppy grass.   The roll was here taken, and only
180 answered out of nearly 500 present on the morning
of the battle.   How many of these were killed and
wounded no one could tell; but it was certain many
must have got separated in the confusion of the evening.
While resting here, we saw pass by, in the crowd of
vehicles and men, a cart laden with commissariat stores,
driven by a man in uniform.   "Food!" cried some one,
and a dozen volunteers jumped up and surrounded the
cart.   The driver tried to whip them off; but he was
pulled off his seat, and the contents of the cart thrown
out in an instant.   They were preserved meats in tins,
which we tore open with our bayonets.   The meat had
been cooked before, I think; at any rate we devoured it.
Shortly after this a general came by with three or four
staff-officers.   He stopped and spoke to our adjutant, and
then rode into the field.   "My lads," said he, "you shall
join my division for the present: fall in, and follow the
regiment that is now passing."   We rose up, fell in by
companies, each about twenty strong, and turned once
more into the stream moving along the road;—regiments,
detachments, single volunteers or militiamen, country
people making off, some with bundles, some without, a
few in carts, but most on foot; here and there wagons
of stores, with men sitting wherever there was room,
others crammed with wounded soldiers.   Many blocks
occurred from horses falling, or carts breaking down and
filling up the road.   In the town the confusion was even
worse, for all the houses seemed full of volunteers and
militiamen, wounded or resting, or trying to find food,
and the streets were almost choked up.   Some officers
were in vain trying to restore order, but the task seemed
a hopeless one.   One or two volunteer regiments which

had arrived from the north the previous night, and had been halted here for orders, were drawn up along the roadside steadily enough, and some of the retreating regiments, including ours, may have preserved the semblance of discipline, but for the most part the mass pushing to the rear was a mere mob. The regulars, or what remained of them, were now, I believe, all in the rear, to hold the advancing enemy in check. A few officers among such a crowd do nothing. To add to the confusion, several houses were being emptied of the wounded brought here the night before, to prevent their falling into the hands of the enemy, some in carts, some being carried to the railway by men. The groans of these poor fellows as they were jostled through the streets went to our hearts, selfish though fatigue and suffering had made us. At last, following the guidance of a staff-officer, who was standing to show the way, we turned off from the main London road and took that towards Kingston. Here the crush was less, and we managed to move along pretty steadily. The air had been cooled by the storm, and there was no dust. We passed through a village where our new general had seized all the public houses, and taken possession of the liquor; and each regiment as it came up was halted, and each man got a drink of beer, served out by companies. Whether the owner got paid I know not, but it was like nectar. It must have been about one o'clock in the afternoon that we came in sight of Kingston. We had been on our legs sixteen hours, and had got over about twelve miles of ground. There is a hill a little south of the Surbiton station, covered then mostly with villas, but open at the western extremity where there was a clump of trees on the summit. We had diverged from the road towards this, and here the general halted us and disposed the line of the division along his front, facing to the south-west, the right of the line reaching down to the Thames, the left extending along the southern slope of the hill, in the direction of the Epsom road by which we had come. We were nearly in the centre, occupying the knoll just in front of the general, who dismounted on the top and tied his horse to a tree. It is not much of a hill, but commands an extensive view over the flat country around; and as we lay wearily on the ground we could see the Thames glistening like a silver field in the bright sunshine, the palace at Hampton Court, the bridge at Kingston, and the old church tower rising above the haze of the town, with the woods of Richmond Park behind it. To most of us the scene could not but call up the associations of happy days of peace—days now ended and peace destroyed through national infatuation. We did not say this to each other, but a deep depression had come upon us, partly due to weakness and fatigue, no doubt, but we saw that another stand was going to be made, and we had no longer any confidence in ourselves. If we could not hold our own when stationary in line, on a good position, but had been broken up into a rabble at the first shock, what chance had we now of manœuvring against a victorious enemy in this open ground? A feeling of desperation came over us, a determination to struggle on against hope; but anxiety for the future of the country, and our friends, and all dear to us, filled our thoughts now that we had time for reflection. We had had no news of any kind since Wood joined us the day before—we knew not what was doing in London, or what the Government was about, or anything else; and exhausted though we were, we felt an intense craving to know what was happening in other parts of the country.

Our general had expected to find a supply of food and ammunition here, but nothing turned up. Most of us had hardly a cartridge left; so he ordered a regiment next to us, which came from the north, and had not been engaged, to give us enough to make up twenty rounds a man, and he sent off a fatigue party to Kingston to try and get provisions, while a detachment of our fellows was allowed to go foraging among the villas in our rear; and in about an hour they brought back some bread and meat, which gave us a slender meal all round. They said most of the houses were empty, and that many had been stripped of all eatables, and a good deal damaged already.

It must have been between three and four o'clock when the sound of cannonading began to be heard in the front, and we could see the smoke of the guns rising above the woods of Esher and Claremont, and soon afterwards some troops emerged from below us. It was the rear-guard of regular troops. There were some guns also, which were driven up the slope and took up their position round the knoll. There were three batteries, but they only counted eight guns amongst them. Behind them was posted the line; it was a brigade apparently of four regiments, but the whole did not look to be more than eight or nine hundred men. Our regiment and another had been moved a little to the rear to make way for them, and presently we were ordered down to occupy the railway station on our right rear. My leg was now so stiff I could no longer march with the rest, and my left arm was very swollen and sore, and almost useless; but anything seemed better than being left behind, so I limped after the battalion as best I could down to the station. There was a goods shed a little in advance of it down the line, a strong brick building, and here my company was posted. The rest of our men lined the wall of the enclosure. A staff-officer came with us to arrange the distribution; we should be supported by line troops, he said; and, in a few minutes, a train full of them came slowly up from Guildford way. It was the last the men got out, the train passed on, and a party began to tear up the rails, while the rest were distributed among the houses on each side. A sergeant's party joined us in our shed, and an engineer officer with sappers came to knock holes in the wall for us to fire from; but there were only half-a-dozen of them, so progress was not rapid, and as we had no tools we could not help.

It was while we were watching this job, that the adjutant, who was as active as ever, looked in, and told us to muster in the yard. The fatigue-party had come from Kingston, and a small baker's handcart of food was made over to us as our share. It contained loaves, flour, and some joints of meat. The meat and the flour we had not time nor means to cook. The loaves we devoured; and there was a tap of water in the yard, so we felt refreshed by the meal. I should have liked to wash my wounds, which were becoming very offensive, but I dared not take off my coat, feeling sure I should not be able to get it on again. It was while we were eating our bread that the rumor first reached us of another disaster, even greater than that we had witnessed ourselves. Whence it came, I know not; but a whisper went down the ranks that Woolwich had been captured. We all knew that it was our only arsenal, and understood the significance of the blow. No hope, if this were true, of saving the country. Thinking over this, we went back to the shed.

Although this was only our second day of war, I think we were already old soldiers, so far that we had come to be careless about fire, and the shot and shell that now began to open on us made no sensation. We felt, indeed, our need of discipline, and we saw plainly enough the slender chance of success coming out of such a rabble as we were; but I think we were all determined

to fight on as long as we could. Our gallant adjutant
gave his spirit to everybody ; and the staff-officer commanding was a very cheery fellow, and went about as if
we were certain of victory. Just as the firing began, he
looked in to say that we were as safe as in a church, that
we must be sure and pepper the enemy well, and that
more cartridges would soon arrive. There were some
steps and benches in the shed, and on these a part of our
men were standing, to fire through the upper loop-holes,
while the line soldiers and others stood on the ground,
guarding the second row. I sat on the floor, for I could
not now use my rifle, and besides, there were more men
than loop-holes. The artillery fire which had opened
now on our position was from a longish range ; and
occupation for the riflemen had hardly begun when there
was a crash in the shed, and I was knocked down by a
blow on the head. I was almost stunned for a time, and
could not make out what had happened. A shot or
shell had hit the shed without quite penetrating the wall,
but the blow had upset the steps resting against it, and
the men standing on them, bringing down a cloud of
plaster and brickbats, one of which had struck me. I felt
now past being of use. I could not use my rifle, and
could barely stand ; and after a time I thought I would
make for my own house, on the chance of finding some
one still there. I got up, therefore, and staggered home-
wards. Musketry fire had now commenced, and our side
were blazing away from the windows of the houses, and
from behind walls, and from the shelter of some trucks
still standing in the station. A couple of field-pieces in
the yard were firing, and in the open space in rear a reserve was drawn up. There, too, was the staff-officer on
horseback, watching the fight through his field-glass. I
remember having still enough sense to feel that the position was a hopeless one. That straggling line of houses

and gardens would surely be broken through at some
point, and then the line must give way like a rope of
sand.

It was about a mile to our house, and I was thinking
how I could possibly drag myself so far when I suddenly
recollected that I was passing Travers's house—one of
the first of a row of villas then leading from the station
to Kingston. Had he been brought home, I wondered,
as his faithful old servant promised, and was his wife
still here? I remember to this day the sensation of
shame I felt, when I recollected that I had not once
given him—my greatest friend—a thought since I carried him off the field the day before. But war and suffering make men selfish. I would go in, now, at any
rate, and rest awhile, and see if I could be of use. The
little garden before the house was as trim as ever—I
used to pass it every day on my way to the train, and
knew every shrub in it—and a blaze of flowers, but the
hall-door stood ajar. I stepped in and saw little Arthur
standing in the hall. He had been dressed as neatly as
ever that day, and as he stood there in his pretty blue
frock and white trousers and socks showing his chubby
little legs, with his golden locks, fair face, and large dark
eyes, the picture of childish beauty, in the quiet hall,
just as it used to look—the vases of flowers, the hat and
coats hanging up, the familiar pictures on the walls—
this vision of peace in the midst of war made me wonder
for a moment, faint and giddy as I was, if the pandemo-
nium outside had any real existence, and was not merely
a hideous dream. But the roar of the guns making the
house shake, and the rushing of the shot, gave a ready
answer. The little fellow appeared almost unconscious
of the scene around him, and was walking up the stairs
holding by the railing, one step at a time, as I had seen
him do a hundred times before, but turned round as I

3*

came in. My appearance frightened him, and staggering as I did into the hall, my face and clothes covered with blood and dirt, I must have looked an awful object to the child, for he gave a cry and turned to run toward the basement stairs. But he stopped on hearing my voice calling him back to his god-papa, and after a while came timidly up to me. Papa had been to the battle, he said, and was very ill: mamma was with papa: Wood was out: Lucy was in the cellar, and had taken him there, but he wanted to go to mamma. Telling him to stay in the hall for a minute till I called him, I climbed up-stairs and opened the bedroom door. My poor friend lay there, his body resting on the bed, his head supported on his wife's shoulder as she sat by the bedside. He breathed heavily, but the pallor of his face, the closed eyes, the prostrate arms, the clammy foam she was wiping from his mouth, all spoke of approaching death. The good old servant had done his duty, at least—he had brought his master home to die in his wife's arms. The poor woman was too intent on her charge to notice the opening of the door, and as the child would be better away, I closed it gently and went down to the hall to take little Arthur to the shelter below, where the maid was hiding. Too late! He lay at the foot of the stairs on his face, his little arms stretched out, his hair dabbled in blood. I had not noticed the crash among the other noises, but a splinter of a shell must have come through the open doorway; it had carried away the back of his head. The poor child's death must have been instantaneous. I tried to lift up the little corpse with my one arm, but even this load was too much for me, and while stooping down I fainted away.

When I came to my senses again it was quite dark, and for some time I could not make out where I was; I lay indeed for some time like one half asleep, feeling no inclination to move. By degrees I became aware that I was on the carpeted floor of a room. All noise of battle had ceased, but there was a sound as of many people close by. At last I sat up and gradually got to my feet. The movement gave me intense pain, for my wounds were now highly inflamed, and my clothes sticking to them made them dreadfully sore. At last I got up and groped my way to the door, and, opening it, at once saw where I was, for the pain had brought back my senses. I had been lying in Travers's little writing-room at the end of the passage, into which I made my way. There was no gas, and the drawing-room door was closed; but from the open dining-room the glimmer of a candle feebly lighted up the hall, in which half a dozen sleeping figures could be discerned, while the room itself was crowded with men. The table was covered with plates, glasses, and bottles; but most of the men were asleep in the chairs or on the floor, a few were smoking cigars, and one or two with their helmets on were still engaged at supper, occasionally grunting out an observation be-tweeen the mouthfuls.

"Sind wackere Soldaten, diese Englischen Freiwilli-gen," said a broad-shouldered brute, stuffing a great hunch of beef into his mouth with a silver fork, an im-plement I should think he must have been using for the first time in his life.

"Ja, ja," replied a comrade, who was lolling back in his chair with a pair of very dirty legs on the table, and one of poor Travers's best cigars in his mouth; "Sie so gut laufen können."

"Ja wohl," responded the first speaker; "aber sind nicht eben so schnell wie die Französischen Mobloten."

"Gewiss," grunted a hulking lout from the floor, lean-ing on his elbow, and sending out a cloud of smoke from his ugly jaws; und da sind hier etwa gute Schützen."

"Hast recht, lange Peter," answered number one; "wenn die Schurken so gut exerciren wie schützen könnten, so wären wir heute nicht hier!"

"Recht! recht!" said the second; "das exerciren macht den guten Soldaten."

What more criticisms on the shortcomings of our unfortunate volunteers might have passed I did not stop to hear, being interrupted by a sound on the stairs. Mrs. Travers was standing on the landing-place; I limped up the stairs to meet her. Among the many pictures of those fatal days engraven on my memory, I remember none more clearly than the mournful aspect of my poor friend, widowed and motherless within a few moments, as she stood there in her white dress, coming forth like a ghost from the chamber of the dead, the candle she held lighting up her face, and contrasting its pallor with the dark hair that fell disordered round it, its beauty radiant even through features worn with fatigue and sorrow. She was calm and even tearless, though the trembling lip told of the effort to restrain the emotion she felt. "Dear friend," she said, taking my hand, "I was coming to seek you; forgive my selfishness in neglecting you so long; but you will understand"—glancing at the door above—"how occupied I have been." "Where," I began, "is"——"my boy?" she answered, anticipating my question. "I have laid him by his father. But now your wounds must be cared for; how pale and faint you look!—rest here a moment,"—and, descending to the dining-room, she returned with some wine, which I gratefully drank, and then, making me sit down on the top step of the stairs, she brought water and linen, and cutting off the sleeve of my coat, bathed and bandaged my wounds. 'Twas I who felt selfish for thus adding to her troubles; but in truth I was too weak to have much will left, and stood in need of the help which she forced me to accept; and the dressing of my wounds afforded indescribable relief. While thus tending me, she explained in broken sentences how matters stood. Every room but her own, and the little parlor into which she with Wood's help had carried me, was full of soldiers. Wood had been taken away to work at repairing the railroad, and Lucy had run off from fright; but the cook had stopped at her post, and had served up supper and opened the cellar for the soldiers' use; she did not understand what they said, and they were rough and boorish, but not uncivil. I should now go, she said, when my wounds were dressed, to look after my own home, where I might be wanted; for herself, she wished only to be allowed to remain watching there—pointing to the room where lay the bodies of her husband and child—where she would not be molested. I felt that her advice was good. I could be of no use as protection, and I had an anxious longing to know what had become of my sick mother and sister; besides, some arrangement must be made for the burial. I therefore limped away. There was no need to express thanks on either side, and the grief was too deep to be reached by any outward show of sympathy.

Outside the house there was a good deal of movement and bustle; many carts going along, the wagoners, from Sussex and Surrey, evidently impressed and guarded by soldiers; and although no gas was burning, the road towards Kingston was well lighted by torches, held by persons standing at short intervals in line, who had been seized for the duty, some of them the tenants of neighboring villas. Almost the first of these torch-bearers I came to was an old gentleman whose face I was well acquainted with, from having frequently traveled up and down in the same train with him. He was a senior clerk in a government office, I believe, and was a mild-looking old man, with a prim face and a long neck, which he used to wrap in a wide, double neckcloth, a thing even in those days seldom seen. Even in that moment of bitterness, I could not help being amused by the absurd figure this poor old fellow presented, with his solemn face and long cravat doing penance with a torch in front of his own door, to light up the path of our conquerors. But a more serious object now presented itself—a corporal's guard passing by, with two English volunteers in charge, their hands tied behind their backs. They cast an imploring glance at me, and I stepped into the road to ask the corporal what was the matter, and even ventured, as he was passing on, to lay my hand on his sleeve. "Auf dem Wege, Spitzbube!" cried the brute, lifting his rifle as if to knock me down. "Must one prisoners who fire at us let shoot," he went on to add; and shot the poor fellows would have been, I suppose, if I had not interceded with an officer who happened to be riding by. "Her Hauptmann," I cried, as loud as I could, "is this your discipline, to let unarmed prisoners be shot without orders?" The officer, thus appealed to, reined in his horse, and halted the guard till he heard what I had to say. My knowledge of other languages here stood me in good stead; for the prisoners, north country factory hands, apparently, were of course utterly unable to make themselves understood, and did not even know in what they had offended. I therefore interpreted their explanation; they had been left behind while skirmishing near Ditton, in a barn, and coming out of their hiding-place in the midst of a party of the enemy, with their rifles in their hands, the latter thought they were going to fire at them from behind. It was a wonder they were not shot down on the spot. The captain heard the tale, and then told the guard to let them go, and they slunk off at once into a by-road. He was a fine soldier-like man, but nothing could exceed the insolence of his manner, which was perhaps all the greater because it seemed not intentional, but to arise from a sense of immeasurable superiority. Between the lame *freiwilliger* pleading for his comrades, and the captain of the conquering army, there was, in his view, an infinite gulf. Had the two men been dogs, their fate could not have been decided more contemptuously. They were let go simply because they were not worth keeping as prisoners, and perhaps to kill any living thing without cause went against the *hauptmann's* sense of justice. But why speak of this insult in particular? Had not every man who lived then his tale to tell of humiliation and degradation? For it was the same story everywhere. After the first stand in line, and when once they had got us on the march, the enemy laughed at us. Our handful of regular troops was sacrificed almost to a man in a vain conflict with numbers; our volunteers and militia, with officers who did not know their work, without ammunition or equipment, or staff to superintend, starving in the midst of plenty, we had soon become a helpless mob, fighting desperately here and there, but with whom, as a manœuvering army, the disciplined invaders did just what they pleased. Happy those whose bones whitened the fields of Surrey; they at least were spared the disgrace we lived to endure. Even you, who have never known what it is to live otherwise than on sufferance, even your cheeks burn when we talk of these days; think, then, what those endured, who, like your grandfather, had been citizens of the proudest nation on earth, which had never known disgrace or defeat, and whose boast it used to be that they bore a flag on which the sun never set! We had heard of generosity in war; we found none; the war was made by us, it was said, and we must take the consequences. London and our only arsenal captured, we were at the mercy of

our captors, and right heavily did they tread on our
necks. Need I tell you the rest?—of the ransom we had
to pay, and the taxes raised to cover it, which keep us
paupers to this day?—the brutal frankness that announced we must give place to a new naval Power, and
be made harmless for revenge?—the victorious troops
living at free quarters, the yoke they put on us made the
more galling that their requisitions had a semblance of
method and legality? Better have been robbed at first
hand by the soldiery themselves, than through our own
magistrates made the instruments for extortion. How
we lived through the degradation we daily and hourly
underwent, I hardly even now understand. And what
was there left to us to live for? Stripped of our colonies;
Canada and the West Indies gone to America; Australia
forced to separate; India lost for ever after the English
there had all been destroyed, vainly trying to hold the
country when cut off from aid by their countrymen; Gib-
raltar and Malta ceded to the new naval Power; Ireland
independent, and in perpetual anarchy and revolution.
When I look at my country as it is now—its trade gone,
its factories silent, its harbors empty, a prey to pauperism and decay—when I see all this, and think what
Great Britain was in my youth, I ask myself whether I
have really a heart or any sense of patriotism that I
should have witnessed such degradation and still care to
live! France was different. There, too, they had to eat
the bread of tribulation under the yoke of the conqueror;
their fall was hardly more sudden or violent than ours;
but war could not take away their rich soil; they had no
colonies to lose; their broad lands, which made their
wealth, remained to them; and they rose again from the
blow. But our people could not be got to see how artificial our prosperity was—that it all rested on foreign
trade and financial credit; that the course of trade once

REMINISCENCES OF A VOLUNTEER.

turned away from us, even for a time, it might never return; and that our credit once shaken, might never be
restored. To hear men talk in those days, you would
have thought that Providence had ordained that our Government should always borrow at three per cent., and
that trade came to us because we lived in a foggy little
island set in a boisterous sea. They could not be got to
see that the wealth heaped up on every side was not
created in the country, but in India and China, and other
parts of the world; and that it would be quite possible
for the people who made money by buying and selling
the natural treasures of the earth, to go and live in other
places, and take their profits with them. Nor would
men believe that there could ever be an end to our coal
and iron, or that they would get to be so much dearer
than the coal and iron of America, that it would no
longer be worth while to work them, and that, therefore,
we ought to insure against the loss of our artificial position as the great centre of trade, by making ourselves
secure, and strong, and respected. We thought we were
living in a commercial millenium, which must last for a
thousand years, at least. After all, the bitterest part of
our reflection is, that all this misery and decay might
have been so easily prevented, and that we brought it
about ourselves by our own shortsighted recklessness.
There, across the narrow straits, was the writing on the
wall, but we would not choose to read it. The warnings
of the few were drowned in the voice of the multitude.
Power was then passing away from the class which had
been used to rule, and to face political dangers, and
which had brought the nation with honor unsullied
through former struggles, into the hands of the lower
classes, uneducated, untrained to the use of political
rights, and swayed by demagogues; and the few who
were wise in their generation, were denounced as alarm-

ists or as aristocrats who sought their own aggrandizement by wasting public money on bloated armaments. The rich were idle and luxurious; the poor grudged the cost of defence. Politics had become a mere bidding for Radical votes, and those who should have led the nation, stooped rather to pander to the selfishness of the day, and humored the popular cry which denounced those who would secure the defence of the nation by enforced arming of its manhood, as interfering with the liberties of the people. Truly the nation was ripe for a fall; but when I reflect how a little firmness and self-denial, or political courage and foresight, might have averted the disaster, I feel that the judgment must have really been deserved. A nation too selfish to defend its liberty, could not have been fit to retain it. To you, my grandchildren, who are now going to seek a new home in a more presperous land, let not this bitter lesson be lost upon you in the country of your adoption. For me, I am too old to begin life again in a strange country; and hard and evil as have been my days, it is not much to await in solitude the time which cannot now be far off, when my old bones will be laid to rest in the soil I have loved so well, and whose happiness and honor I have so long survived.